PUFFIN BOOKS

DIARY OF A WIMPY KID

THE MELTDOWN

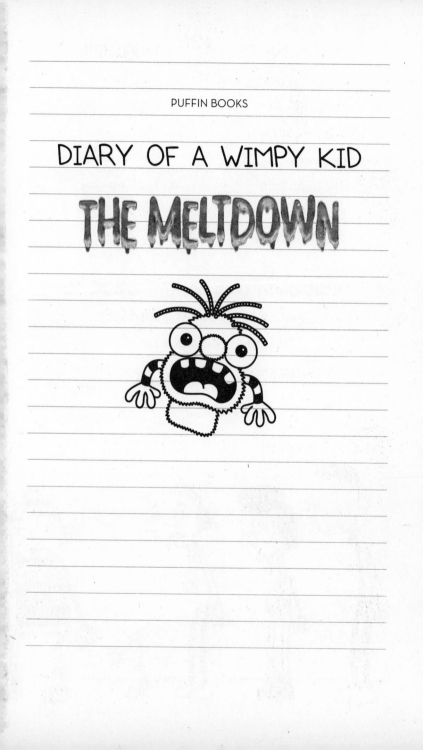

THE *DIARY OF A WIMPY KID* SERIES

MORE *DIARY OF A WIMPY KID* BOOKS

DIARY
of a
Wimpy Kid

THE MELTDOWN

by Jeff Kinney

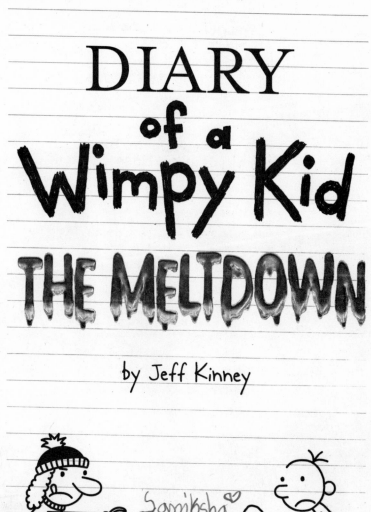

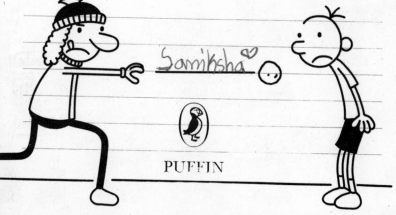

PUFFIN

PUFFIN BOOKS

UK | USA | Canada | Ireland | Australia
India | New Zealand | South Africa

Puffin Books is part of the Penguin Random House group of companies whose
addresses can be found at global.penguinrandomhouse.com.

www.penguin.co.uk   www.puffin.co.uk   www.ladybird.co.uk

First published in the English language in the USA
by Amulet Books, an imprint of ABRAMS, 2018
Original English title: *Diary of a Wimpy Kid: The Meltdown*
(All rights reserved in all countries by Harry N. Abrams, Inc.)
Published simultaneously in Great Britain by Puffin Books 2018

001

Book design by Jeff Kinney
Cover design by Chad W. Beckerman and Jeff Kinney

The moral right of the author/illustrator has been asserted

Printed and bound in India by Replika Press Pvt. Ltd.

A CIP catalogue record for this book is available from the British Library

HARDBACK
ISBN: 978-0-241-32198-0

INTERNATIONAL HARDBACK
ISBN: 978-0-141-37820-6

All correspondence to:
Puffin Books, Penguin Random House Children's
80 Strand, London WC2R ORL

TO DEB

JANUARY

<u>Monday</u>

Everybody in my neighbourhood is outside today enjoying the warm weather and sunshine. Well, everyone except ME. It's kind of hard to enjoy a heat wave when it's the middle of the WINTER.

People are calling this "wacky weather", but it just doesn't feel right. Maybe I'm old-fashioned, but I think it should be cold in the winter and hot in the SUMMER.

I've heard the whole PLANET is warming up, and that human beings are the reason. But don't blame ME, because I just GOT here.

If the world IS getting hotter, I just hope it doesn't happen too FAST. Because if things keep up at THIS rate I'll be riding a camel to high school.

They say the ice caps are melting and the sea is rising, so I've been trying to convince Mom and Dad to buy a house higher up on our hill. But they just don't seem all that concerned.

It kind of makes me nervous that I'm the only one in my family worried about this stuff. Because if we don't do something about the situation SOON we're gonna wish we DID.

It's not just the rising sea levels I'm nervous about. Those ice caps have been around for millions of years, and there could be things buried inside them that should STAY that way.

I saw a movie about a caveman who got frozen in ice, and when it melted thousands of years later he was still ALIVE. I don't know if that kind of thing could actually happen in real life, but if there ARE unfrozen cavemen walking around these days the night janitor at my school might be one of them.

SPLOP

If we DO figure a way out of this climate mess, it's probably gonna be someone from MY generation who solves it. That's why I'm always nice to the SMART kids, because THEY'RE the ones who are gonna save our butts.

NERD!

SHOVE

Whatever the answer is, I guarantee you TECHNOLOGY is gonna be the key.

Grown-ups are always saying that too much technology is BAD for kids, but I say the more the BETTER.

In fact, as soon as I can afford one of those high-tech toilets that learns all your habits I'm gonna get the most expensive model.

Some people worry that one day we'll lose control of our technology and robots will take OVER.

Well, if that happens, I'm gonna make sure I'm on THEIR side.

I've actually been PREPARING for when the robots take over by sucking up to the appliances in my house.

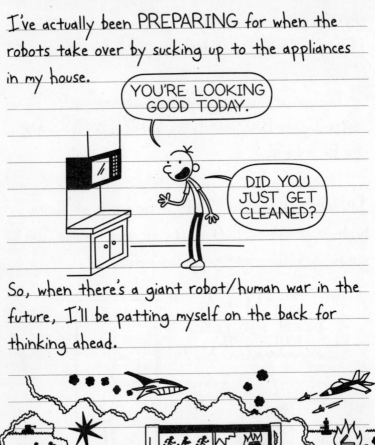

So, when there's a giant robot/human war in the future, I'll be patting myself on the back for thinking ahead.

My brother Rodrick says that in the future
people will have robot body parts, and we'll all be
CYBORGS.

Well, I hope I don't have to wait too long for
that, because if I could buy myself a pair of
robot legs I could get a half-hour of extra sleep
each morning.

I guess we don't really know what's gonna happen
in the future. And you could drive yourself CRAZY
worrying about it.

Even if we solve all the problems we have right
now, some NEW thing will come along, and then
we'll have to deal with THAT.

I've read that's what happened with the
DINOSAURS. They were riding high for a
couple of hundred million years, and then an
asteroid came and wiped them out.

What's really crazy is that cockroaches were around
back then, and somehow THEY survived. And
they'll probably be here long after we're gone, too.
Personally, I think cockroaches are disgusting. But
they must be doing SOMETHING right.

SMACK

Speaking of SURVIVAL, right now I'm just trying to get through middle school. And the last few days haven't been all that great.

Even though it's warm outside, the thermostat at school still thinks it's WINTER. So the furnace is on full blast all day, which makes it hard to concentrate in class.

And it's worse in the CAFETERIA because there aren't any windows you can open to get fresh air.

The heat has been frying my brain, and I've been forgetting when my homework is due. I forgot a really BIG one today, which was my country project for the International Showcase.

Back in November, everyone had to choose a country to do a report on. I picked Italy because I'm a HUGE pizza fan.

But it turns out Italy was a really popular choice, so my Social Studies teacher had to draw names to decide who got it. And she chose Dennis Tracton, which isn't fair because he's lactose intolerant and can't even eat cheese.

So the teacher assigned me Malta, which I didn't even know was a country.

Anyway, that was two months ago, and I didn't give my country project a second thought until TODAY. And the only reason I remembered was because when I got to school everybody was wearing weird clothes.

I probably should've realized it was International Showcase day when my friend Rowley came to get me for school wearing a crazy get-up. But he's ALWAYS doing strange stuff, so I barely even noticed.

In homeroom I took a look at Rowley's project to see how much work was involved, and that's when I started to panic.

His report looked like it took a TON of time, and it was pretty obvious his parents helped him with it. Of course Rowley had actually BEEN to the country he got assigned, so I'm sure that made it a lot EASIER for him.

I asked Rowley to be a pal and switch countries with me, but he's kind of selfish so he wouldn't go for it. That meant I was on my own, and I only had a few hours to do my whole project from SCRATCH. And I didn't know WHERE I was gonna find a tri-fold board this late in the game.

That's when I remembered that I had a tri-fold in my LOCKER. I had started my country project the day after it was assigned so I could get ahead with things for once. But, when I pulled it out to see how FAR I'd got, I was pretty disappointed.

	MYSTERIOUS **MAL**	

This project was 50% of my Social Studies grade, so I was desperate. I tried getting help from my CLASSMATES, but all THAT did was remind me I need to get some smarter friends.

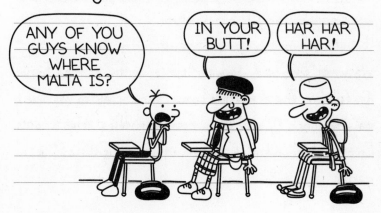

I stayed indoors for recess to work on my project. I didn't have time to go down to the library for research, so I had to do a lot of GUESSING. The only thing I felt pretty sure about was that Malta was near Russia, but I was pretty shaky on everything ELSE.

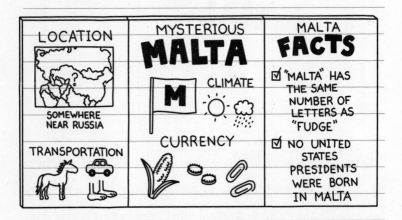

LOCATION

SOMEWHERE NEAR RUSSIA

TRANSPORTATION

MYSTERIOUS **MALTA**

M

CLIMATE

CURRENCY

MALTA **FACTS**

☑ "MALTA" HAS THE SAME NUMBER OF LETTERS AS "FUDGE"

☑ NO UNITED STATES PRESIDENTS WERE BORN IN MALTA

Once I finished filling out my tri-fold, I started working on the OTHER stuff.

We were supposed to wear our country's "traditional dress" for the International Showcase, so on the way to lunch I picked out some clothes from the Lost and Found in front of the principal's office.

Luckily, there were a few decent items in the box, and I put together an outfit that looked pretty convincing.

Everyone was supposed to bring in a traditional MEAL, too. At lunch I bought as many items as I could afford and threw something together that seemed like it might've come from another country.

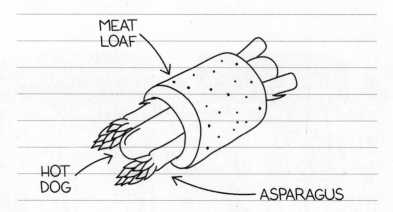

MEAT LOAF

HOT DOG

ASPARAGUS

The International Showcase was during the last period, and when I set up my project in the gym I was actually feeling pretty good about things. But I wish I'd got assigned a country where they wore lighter clothes, because the furnace was still on full blast.

The heat was getting to some OTHER kids, too, and tempers were starting to flare. At one point Brazil and Bulgaria got in a fight over table space, and a teacher had to come and break it up.

Kids came in from the elementary school to check out our projects and ask questions. But all I had to do to get them to move along was pretend I only spoke Maltese.

After that, the PARENTS started to arrive. Luckily, MINE couldn't come because Dad was at work and Mom was at her college. But some kid in my grade has a mom and dad who are actually FROM Malta, which was really bad luck for ME.

I thought they were gonna report me to my teacher, and I was ready to make a run for it. But then something happened that let me off the hook.

The fight that started between Brazil and Bulgaria flared back up and spilled over to the "C" and "D" countries. And before long the whole GYM was at war.

Luckily, the bell rang, and school got dismissed before anyone was seriously hurt. But the whole situation doesn't exactly give me a lot of hope for world peace.

Tuesday

Well, I THOUGHT I was in the clear, but I was wrong. My Social Studies teacher sent a note home to my parents that said I had to do my International Showcase project AGAIN.

So Mom said I can't watch TV or play video games until I finish. I figure I can probably get this thing done by Saturday, but it won't matter anyway. That's because Mom is making me and my brothers have "Screen-Free Weekends".

Mom thinks us kids are addicted to screens, and they're the reason we misbehave. So she started this new policy where we're not allowed to use any electronics on Saturdays and Sundays, and we have to find other ways to entertain ourselves.

What really stinks is that when Mom catches
us BEHAVING at the weekends she thinks it's
PROOF that Screen-Free Weekends are working.

So lately me and Rodrick have been remembering to
MISBEHAVE on Saturdays and Sundays so Mom
doesn't think her no-screens policy is working.
And MANNY joins in, too, because I guess he
likes to do whatever his big brothers are doing.

Mom says kids these days don't know how to interact with one another because we're always staring at our screens. So she's been working with me and Rodrick on our "social skills".

One thing Mom's always trying to get me to do is look her in the eye when I'm talking to her. I can do that for a LITTLE while, but after a few seconds it just gets too weird.

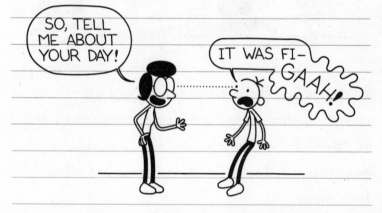

The latest thing Mom's been making me do is practise shaking hands with Dad. But that's awkward for BOTH of us.

Mom wants me to "branch out" and make more friends in the neighbourhood. But I'm already friends with ROWLEY, and he's all I can really handle right now.

Even though there are a ton of kids on my street, I really can't see being friends with any of them. I ALREADY feel like I'm making an exception for Rowley, and the options go downhill from there.

Our house is halfway up Surrey Street, and Rowley's house is near the top. Sometimes it's a pain to even go and see HIM because I have to pass by FREGLEY'S house to do it. And nine times out of ten Fregley is hanging out in his front yard.

Across the street from Fregley is Jacob Hoff, but he almost never comes outside because his parents are always making him practise the clarinet. And on either side of Jacob are Ernesto Gutierrez and Gabriel Johns, who are in my grade.

Ernesto and Gabriel are nice kids and all, but they BOTH have bad breath, so those two are perfect for each other.

Two doors down from me is David Marsh, who's really into karate. He's best friends with Joseph O'Rourke, who's always doing something to get himself injured.

Next door to Joseph is Mitchell Pickett, who makes a killing selling pre-made snowballs in the winter. And, mark my words, one day that kid's gonna be a MILLIONAIRE.

Mitchell lives next to a boy one year younger than me who everybody calls Speed Bump. But people steer clear of him because his two older brothers are already in jail.

There's a kid named Pervis Gentry who has a tree house in his backyard, and he spends his summers solving neighbourhood crimes. But most of the time the person responsible is Speed Bump.

There's a duplex building three quarters of the way down the hill, and the two families who live in it HATE each other.

I can never get the kids in that house straight, but I know one of them is named Gino because he has a tattoo on his arm, even though he's only something like seven years old.

There's a boy who lives with his grandmother a few doors down, and his name is Gibson.

Everyone calls him Baby Gibson, because no matter how much time goes by he never seems to get any OLDER. For all I know, Baby Gibson is thirty-two years old and he's got kids of his OWN.

There's a playgroup of pre-schoolers that gets together twice a week at Mrs Jimenez's house. I don't know which kids are HERS and which ones are her FRIENDS'. What I DO know is that those kids are totally out of control, and the moms don't really seem to care.

There are some older kids on our street, too. Anthony Denard is a sophomore in high school, and he just started shaving. But he got carried away with the razor blade and accidentally shaved off one of his eyebrows.

Anthony drew it back on with a brown marker, but he didn't do a good job, and now one half of his face always looks surprised.

Anthony's best friend is Sheldon Reyes, who tried to make money ploughing the neighbours' driveways the first time it snowed this winter.

But Sheldon doesn't have his licence yet, and he did a lot of damage in our neighbourhood before his dad found out his son was using his truck.

A few doors down from me are the Garza twins,
Jeremy and Jameson, who made up their own
language when they were toddlers. And when
those two are together no one can understand a
word they say.

There are a bunch of GIRLS on my street, too,
but they're just as bad as the GUYS.

The Marlee sisters live across from Rowley's house, and all five of them were born within a few years of each other. I don't know what their deal is, but those girls will just randomly attack people who come into their yard.

Emilia Greenwall lives a few doors down from the Marlee sisters. Emilia always dresses like a princess, and I think she's seen too many Disney movies.

Latricia Hooks lives in the bungalow across from
the duplex, and she's a six-foot-two high-school
junior. Rodrick won't go anywhere NEAR Latricia
because she used to bully him when he was MY age.

Latricia's sister Victoria is in love with Ernesto
Gutierrez for some reason, and Victoria's best
friend, Evelyn Trimble, dresses like a vampire.

In fact, I'm pretty sure Evelyn thinks she IS
a vampire, which is one reason I'm glad I don't
take the bus any more.

I haven't even mentioned HALF the kids who live on my hill. But if I went down the whole list it'd take FOREVER.

Mom always asks me why I'm not friends with any kids at the BOTTOM of the hill, even though I've told her a million times why that'll never HAPPEN.

Surrey Street is divided into two halves. There's UPPER Surrey Street, which is the hill, and LOWER Surrey Street, which is the flat part at the bottom.

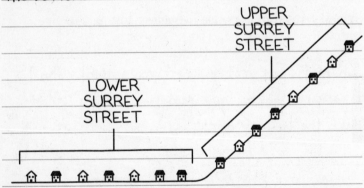

UPPER SURREY STREET

LOWER SURREY STREET

And, even though we all live on the same street, the hill kids and the non-hill kids can't STAND one another.

Living on the hill is no fun. First of all, it's really far from the school, and that last stretch at the end of the day is no joke. ESPECIALLY when it's hot like it has been lately.

The worst thing about living on a hill is that there's not a lot you can DO on it. And if you want to play with a ball you can forget about it.

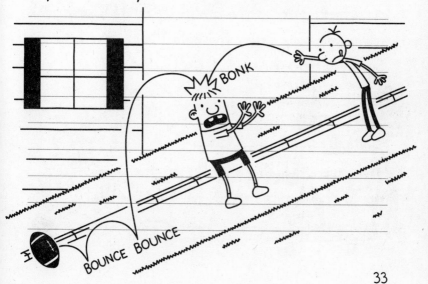

BONK

BOUNCE BOUNCE

But the kids who live at the BOTTOM of the hill have it MADE. Their part of the street is FLAT, so they can do anything they want down there. That's why all the athletes come from LOWER Surrey Street.

The thing is, the kids who live at the bottom of our street think they OWN it. And, if any of us hill people come down there to PLAY, the Lower Surrey Street kids won't LET us.

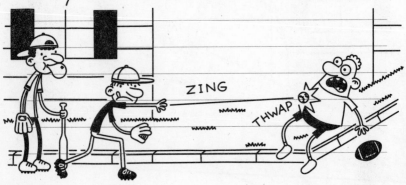

ZING

THWAP

In fact, the reason it took me four years to learn to ride a bike was because I had to do it in five-second spurts.

But when it SNOWS the tables are turned. All of a sudden the Lower Surrey Street kids want to use our hill for SLEDGING, but that's when we give those guys a taste of their own medicine.

35

Most of the time we can keep the Lower Surrey Street kids off the hill. But they're SNEAKY, and sometimes they slip past us.

Last winter a bunch of the Lower Surrey Street kids bought the same winter gear as the hill kids, and it was WEEKS before any of us caught on.

If you live on Surrey Street, you're either a HILL kid or a NON-hill kid, and there's no switching sides.

There's a kid named Trevor Nix who lived on the hill until last summer, which is when his family moved to a bigger house at the bottom of the street.

But the kids down there still consider Trevor a HILL person, so they won't let him play on the street. Us hill kids think of him as a traitor for moving, and we won't let him sledge in the winter. So now Trevor is basically stuck indoors year-round.

There's a lot of bad blood between the Upper Surrey Street kids and the Lower Surrey Street kids, which is why we can't be friends. But whenever I try to explain the situation to Mom she just doesn't get it.

In fact, NONE of the moms on our street do. They're all friends with each other, and they have no CLUE about what's REALLY going on.

Lately, though, things have been pretty calm on our street. Us hill kids keep to OUR side, and the other guys keep to THEIRS. But if someone does something stupid this whole place is gonna BLOW.

<u>Sunday</u>
The temperature dropped about ten degrees over
the weekend, so today my family was out looking
for our pet pig.

For the Christmas holidays, my family went away
and we left the pig in a kennel. But I guess the
pig thought it should've come WITH us, and it
wasn't too happy about being left behind.

When we got back HOME, the pig let us know
how it felt about not being included on our family
holiday.

After a few days of the pig acting out, Dad
decided enough was enough, and he sent it to
"obedience school". But the next morning we got
a call from the lady who runs the place, and she
said our pig ESCAPED.

We've been putting up signs asking for help finding our lost pig ever since. But that thing is SMART, so I don't think it's LOST. It just doesn't want to be FOUND.

I figure the pig is probably off HIBERNATING somewhere. Mom says pigs don't do that, but, if you ask me, I think they SHOULD.

If I was an animal, that's EXACTLY what I'D be doing right now. On the last day of the autumn, I think everyone should get into their pyjamas and check out until the spring.

When I was younger, I actually TRIED to hibernate, but it didn't work.

I used to get SUPER excited for Christmas, and once December rolled around it was really hard for me to wait until the big day.

So one year on December 1st I told my parents I was gonna go to sleep, and that they shouldn't wake me up until Christmas morning. I was pretty surprised when they didn't put up a fight.

I went to bed that night, but I only slept until 1:30 p.m. the next day. Then my sleep schedule was screwed up for the next two weeks.

Mom says it's IMPOSSIBLE for human beings to hibernate, but I'm not 100% convinced that's TRUE.

There's this group of wild kids who live in the woods, and everyone calls them the Mingos. You never see the Mingos in the WINTER, and when they make their first appearance in the SPRING they look like they just woke up.

So, if they're not HIBERNATING, I don't know WHAT they're doing all winter.

The rest of us NORMAL people have to grind it out and deal with the cold weather.

And the only way to do THAT is to stay inside as much as possible and keep warm.

When we got back from our trip a few weeks ago, there was a package on our front step. It was a Christmas gift from Aunt Dorothy, and when we opened it there was a giant BLANKET inside.

That thing was AMAZING. It was really soft, but it was also HEAVY, which is exactly how I like my blankets. The only problem was that the gift was for all three of us boys, and we started fighting over it right away.

We wanted to use the blanket at the same time, so Mom told us we were gonna have to take TURNS with it.

But the three of us have never been any good at SHARING, so Mom had to make a blanket schedule that spelled out who got to use it when.

Blanket Schedule

6:00 P.M.	7:30 P.M.	9:00 P.M.
Manny	Manny	Manny
6:30 P.M.	8:00 P.M.	9:30 P.M.
Greg	Greg	Greg
7:00 P.M.	8:30 P.M.	10:00 P.M.
Rodrick	Rodrick	Rodrick

But that wasn't really FAIR. Manny has his OWN blanket, so he was being greedy.

When it was MY turn to use the blanket, I tried to make the most of it.

But it was really hard to enjoy myself because Rodrick would start hovering over me when I still had fifteen minutes left on my shift.

We each got three half-hour shifts a night, but Rodrick would cheat Manny out of HIS turn by taking the blanket into the bathroom right before Manny's shift was supposed to START. Then Rodrick would sit in there for an HOUR, which cut into MY shift.

POUND
POUND

So Mom made a rule that we can't take the blanket into the bathroom.

One night I slept with the blanket in my room, and Rodrick complained because he wanted to use it while he ate breakfast. Mom made a NEW rule that said if you slept with the blanket it had to be returned downstairs by 8:00 a.m.

By the end of the first week, there were so many rules that Mom had to put them all in a MANUAL, which ended up being something like twenty-five pages long.

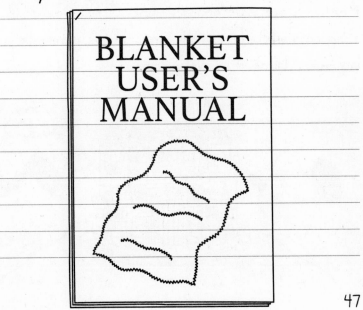

But THAT didn't solve our problems, and eventually Mom took the blanket away to give it to someone who "deserved" it. She said it was our fault we couldn't have something nice because we didn't know how to SHARE.

Grown-ups are always talking about how great sharing is, but personally I think it's overrated. And if I ever get enough money I'm gonna build a big castle all for myself, and there's gonna be a big heavy blanket in every room.

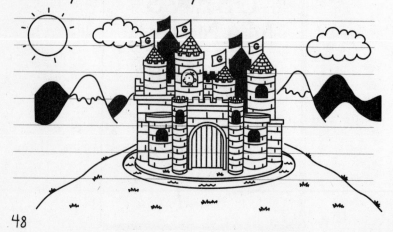

<u>Monday</u>
When I woke up this morning, it was below
freezing outside. I was relieved it actually felt like
WINTER again, but when Mom told me I had to
wear thermal underwear to school I thought maybe
global warming isn't such a bad thing after all.

I HATE wearing thermal underwear because it's
uncomfortable and I feel RIDICULOUS wearing
it. Thermal underwear looks cool when it's on the
mannequin at the mall, but when I put it on I
just look like a retired superhero.

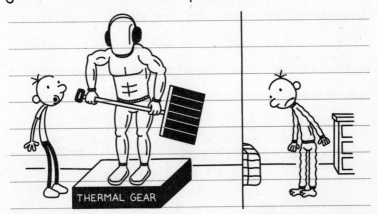

THERMAL GEAR

The mannequins at the mall are always super buff,
and they make guys like me who can't spend three
hours in the gym every day look bad.

If I ever get in really good shape, I'm gonna sign up to be a mannequin model. Because that would be an awesome thing to brag about on a date.

The mannequins you see at the sports store are always in athletic poses, and it looks like it would be HARD to stay in that position while someone sculpts you. And that's just too much effort for a job that should be EASY.

So when I apply for the job I'm gonna do it at the bed store.

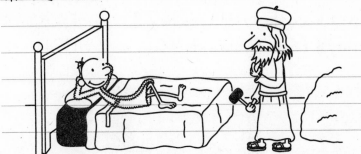

Mom says I'm LUCKY to have thermal underwear, because our ANCESTORS didn't have this kind of stuff to keep them warm.

Sometimes I WONDER about my ancestors, though. I have no idea why they chose to live HERE when they could've picked somewhere a whole lot WARMER.

But I can't complain, because they SURVIVED and everything they did led directly to ME. I just wish they could see how I turned out so they'd know all their sacrifices were WORTH it.

I guess we're ALL lucky to be here, because human beings have had to go through a LOT to get to where we are now.

At school we learned that 10,000 years ago a big sheet of ice covered half the planet. And if people made it through THAT I guess we can get through ANYTHING.

My teacher said that one day the Earth is gonna be in another ice age and the glaciers will come back, but I hope it doesn't happen any time SOON.

I've heard glaciers move SLOWLY, which is a good thing. Because maybe we'll have a chance to DO something about it.

I don't know which is worse, a planet that's too HOT or one that's too COLD. All I know is that today it was cold, and it wasn't fun walking to school in the morning.

I tried to cheer myself up by thinking of things I LIKE about the winter, but I came up with a really short list. Christmas is great and all, but after that it's just a long slog to the spring.

I've decided the only thing that actually makes winter worth it is the HOT CHOCOLATE. I used to be on the Safety Patrols, and I'd get free hot chocolate at school. But after I got kicked off I had to start bringing my OWN.

Lately I've been filling a thermos with hot chocolate every morning, and that keeps me warm on the walk to school.

But today Dad must've grabbed MY thermos and left me with HIS. And I didn't realize what had happened until I took a giant gulp of cream of mushroom soup.

I wish Mom and Dad would drive me to school in the morning, but they leave a half-hour before I do.

There are some kids on my hill whose parents drive
them in on cold days like today. But when me
and Rowley try to flag them down to hitch a
ride they won't even make eye contact. And that
really stinks, because us hill kids are supposed to
have each other's BACKS.

It was so cold out today that the teachers
decided to keep us indoors for recess, which was
perfectly fine with ME.

The LAST time we had outdoor recess on a day like
today Albert Sandy was saying it was so cold that
your spit would freeze before it hit the GROUND.

Well, it turns out he was WRONG, and recess that day was a total NIGHTMARE.

Usually indoor recess isn't much fun. We're supposed to play board games and do arts and crafts, but kids always get restless and find ways to liven things up.

So today our teacher said we were gonna try something NEW.

She taught us how to play a game called "Museum", where everyone has to freeze like a statue and hold still for as long as possible.

It was actually pretty FUN, but when recess ended I realized it was just an easy way to get us to BEHAVE for a half-hour.

The thing I don't like about being indoors at school in the winter is that a lot of kids are SICK, and I really don't want someone getting ME sick.

Our school is FULL of germs, and NOBODY covers their mouth when they cough or sneeze.

Walking down the hallway between classes is like walking through a war zone.

Nobody remembers to sneeze into the crook of their arm, and kids like Albert Sandy aren't HELPING things. Today at lunch Albert told a story about a guy who covered his sneeze, and when he did he blew his head clean OFF.

I told Albert his story wasn't true, but he swore it WAS. He said the guy actually SURVIVED, and now he works as a grocery bagger at the local supermarket.

Albert's ALWAYS spreading bad information like that, and the kids at my table believe every word he says. So now there's ZERO chance any of these guys will cover their mouths the next time they have to sneeze.

A couple of weeks ago Albert said that when someone's pet dies in the winter they have to wait until the ground thaws in the spring before it can be buried. He said they need somewhere to KEEP their pets in the meantime.

Albert said the people in our town use the school cafeteria's walk-in freezer to store their pets for the winter, and that right now it's full to CAPACITY.

I'm almost POSITIVE this is just another one of Albert's stupid made-up stories. But until we find our PIG I'm not gonna order the Pork Barbecue Special, just in case.

I'm seriously thinking of changing lunch tables, because I'm tired of sitting with Albert Sandy and all these other idiots every day. One kid I won't miss is Teddy Silvetti, who wears the same sweater all winter long.

Teddy's sweater has NEVER been cleaned, and there are food stains all over it. Sometimes the kids at my table try to guess what each stain IS, which is what they were doing today.

See, this is the reason girls at my school have pictures of pop singers in their lockers. The guys in my grade just aren't giving them any good OPTIONS.

I can't even IMAGINE how many germs are on Teddy's sweater, which is why I sit at least two seats away from him.

Most of my brain power at school goes on keeping tabs on whose germs are WHERE. And I've already filled up two notebooks this winter.

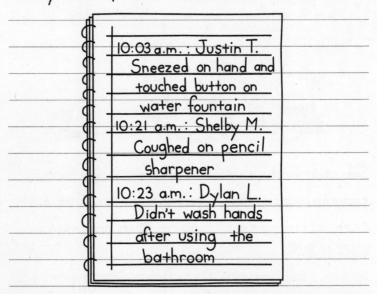

10:03 a.m.: Justin T. Sneezed on hand and touched button on water fountain

10:21 a.m.: Shelby M. Coughed on pencil sharpener

10:23 a.m.: Dylan L. Didn't wash hands after using the bathroom

The times it gets tricky is when you have TWINS like Jeremy and Jameson Garza. I can't tell them apart, and today it looked to me like one was sick but the other one WASN'T.

COUGH

So I shot a spitball into the sick one's hair to make it easier to keep track of him.

The only GOOD thing about being ill is the cherry lozenges Mom gives me when I have a sore throat. I know you're supposed to suck on them real slow, but I chew those things like CANDY, and I go through a few packs a day.

The girls in my grade LOVE the smell of cherry lozenges, which almost makes being ill WORTH it.

Unfortunately, the GUYS in my grade like the smell, too. And they're always trying to get me to GIVE them some.

A few weeks ago I thought I felt a sore throat coming on, and I brought three packs of cherry lozenges to school with me. I kept one pack in my pocket and the OTHER two in my locker.

But Jake McGough sniffed out the packs I was keeping in my locker, and by the time I found out Speed Bump had already picked the lock.

I wish I didn't have to go to school at ALL during cold and flu season. Maybe one day I'll buy one of those big plastic bubbles so I'm not exposed to other kids' germs.

But I'm sure my bubble wouldn't last a DAY before some jerk popped it.

Even though I hate being ill, I'm kind of glad they haven't come up with a cure for the cold yet.

Because if they DID I wouldn't be able to fake being ill and stay home from school to play video games.

Today it was even colder on the walk HOME than it was on the walk to school. And this time me and Rowley were facing the WIND, which made it ten times WORSE.

CHATTER
CHATTER

CHATTER
CHATTER

It was so bad that we had to make a few pit stops on the way home. The first place we ducked into was the pizza shop, because there's a big oven in there, so it's always warm inside. But when the guy who owns the place realized we weren't gonna BUY anything he kicked us out.

Our next stop was the town library. That's a public building, and I knew they couldn't tell us to leave. But when the librarians started getting pushy with the books we left on our OWN.

I wish we'd used the bathroom in the library before we headed back outside, though, because when we got halfway home Rowley really needed to go. We knocked on a few doors, but when people saw us they pretended they weren't home.

KNOCK
KNOCK

We finally got someone to ANSWER, but by
that point Rowley's face was so frozen he couldn't
even form WORDS.

By the time we got to Surrey Street, I thought
Rowley was gonna have a medical emergency. But
I knew none of the Lower Surrey Street people
were gonna let us inside their houses.

There's a big ROCK in Mr Yee's front yard,
and I told Rowley he should duck behind it to do
his business. Personally, I wouldn't pee outside in
THIS kind of cold because Albert Sandy told us a
story about what happened to a guy who DID.

But I didn't feel like it was the right time to mention that to Rowley, and I'm not really sure he had to do a number ONE, anyway.

Whatever he was doing back there, he was taking FOREVER. Some of the Lower Surrey Street kids came out of their houses to play, and before long Rowley had drawn a crowd. I just backed off because I really didn't want people to know I was WITH him.

ZUFF WHUZ WHUFF WHOO WHOOO!

Thankfully, Rowley wrapped things up and we got out of there before anyone realized what he was DOING. Because this is just the sort of stupid thing that could end up sparking a WAR.

Tuesday

It was seriously cold again this morning, so I dug my scarf and a pair of old gloves out of the wardrobe. Mom said I should wear the mittens Gramma knitted for me last winter, but when she made those things she forgot to add the THUMBS.

KNIT
KNIT

So, whenever I put them on, it's basically like wearing SOCKS on my hands. And they're totally USELESS in a snowball fight.

FAH!

BAP

Mom said I should wear earmuffs, too, but the thing I've learned is that, if kids know you can't hear them COMING, you're just ASKING for it.

STEP STEP STEP STEP

The reason I get so cold is because I'm SKINNY and I don't have any insulation. Every winter I try to eat a lot to give myself an extra layer of blubber. But I guess I've got a fast metabolism, because nothing I do ever seems to WORK.

I think it was something like minus ten degrees outside this morning, and on the walk to school I started wondering if a person's BLOOD could freeze.

I've heard people are something like 60% WATER, so I guess it's POSSIBLE. But it kind of feels like something Albert Sandy would make up.

What I was worried about the MOST was FROSTBITE. By the time I was halfway to school, my ears were STINGING, and I really wished I had listened to Mom about the earmuffs.

I thought one of my ears might actually fall OFF, and that I wouldn't notice until I was in class.

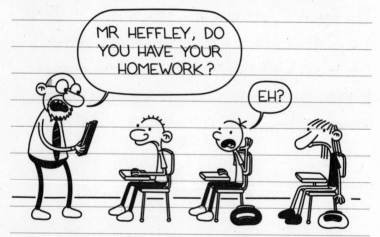

It wasn't just my EARS I was worried about, though. Apparently there are a LOT of body parts where you can get frostbite.

I wouldn't want to lose my NOSE because I'd look a little freaky without one. Then again, my desk in Social Studies is right next to the BATHROOM, so at least THAT situation would get a little better.

Plus, my nose ALWAYS runs on cold days, and I never realize I've got frozen snot on my face until it's too late.

I'd like to hang on to my LIPS, too, because if I didn't have them it would always look like I was SMILING. And in certain situations that could be a real problem.

I was lucky I found those GLOVES because I wouldn't want to lose any FINGERS, either. The only thing I'd be willing to give up is my pinky toes, because I hardly EVER use them. The last time I can remember using them was when I was in pre-school and I needed to count to twenty. But, other than that, I'm drawing a blank.

I guess a lot of OTHER kids were worried about frostbite, too, because when I got to school there was a whole line of boys in the bathroom waiting to use the hand dryer. And that made me five minutes late for first period.

It wasn't as windy on the walk home today, but it was just as COLD. Me and Rowley stopped at the pizza place again to warm up, because Rowley found a coupon for two free meatball subs in his coat pocket.

After we left the pizza place, we still had a long way to walk. But that's when I had an idea.

My gramma's house is halfway between our school and Surrey Street, and I knew there was no one HOME. That's because Gramma goes down south each winter and doesn't come back until the spring.

During the winter Gramma sends us pictures of herself and her friends in their bathing suits to let us know that she's having a good time.

Gramma takes her dog, Sweetie, with her, too. So, while I'm freezing my butt off up here, it's great to know Sweetie is lying on a beach down south soaking up the sun.

Gramma usually keeps a key inside her garden gnome right next to the front door. And, sure enough, that's EXACTLY where it was today.

I figured we could use Gramma's house to warm up in before the last push home. Rowley was nervous about us going inside with no adults home, but I told him Gramma was FAMILY, and she'd WANT me to use her house while she was away.

When we walked in, I was pretty surprised. It was like a FREEZER in there, so I guess Gramma turns down the thermostat for the winter.

Usually Gramma CRANKS up the heat. When she's home, it's so warm that you have to eat your ice-cream sandwich with the freezer drawer open or the ice cream will melt in your hands.

The first thing I did when we got inside Gramma's was turn up the thermostat. It was taking a while for the house to heat up, though, so I turned on the oven and we warmed up in a HURRY.

Gramma had a bunch of snacks in her refrigerator, and me and Rowley helped ourselves. But while we were eating we saw some MOVEMENT outside the front window.

It was Mrs McNeil, Gramma's snoopy next-door neighbour. She must've noticed the light from the fridge, and now she was trying to see inside.

We stayed out of sight, and eventually Mrs McNeil went away. But now I knew we had to be CAREFUL, because I really didn't need her calling the COPS. So we got down low and went into the living room, where Gramma has her TV.

Gramma has ALL the cable channels, and luckily she didn't shut THOSE down for the winter. But we couldn't risk attracting Mrs McNeil again, so we put a blanket over ourselves AND the television and watched it THAT way.

I guess we kind of lost track of time, because when we shut off the TV it was DARK out. By now it was nice and toasty in Gramma's house, and I really didn't wanna go back out there in the cold. So I had an idea for how to make the walk home a little more COMFORTABLE.

I figured if we warmed up our clothes in Gramma's dryer before we headed back out it would take the edge off for the rest of the trip. So we went down to the basement where Gramma keeps her laundry machines and put in our clothes.

We set the timer to thirty minutes and waited.
But it was a little awkward hanging out in our
underwear while the dryer did its thing.

Plus, it was COLD in the basement, so we looked
around for something to WEAR. Rowley found
a sweatshirt I gave Gramma for her birthday
and he put THAT on. But I didn't feel RIGHT
wearing Gramma's clothes.

I found a sweater that Gramma knitted for Sweetie, and it fitted better than I expected. But it was a little ITCHY, and I couldn't remember if Sweetie ever had FLEAS.

But, while I was looking around for something to swap it with, we heard NOISES upstairs.

My FIRST thought was that Gramma had given Mrs McNeil a key to the house, and now she was inside. But Rowley said it might be a BURGLAR who knew no one was home, and I thought maybe he was RIGHT.

We heard some more stomping around upstairs, and when the door to the basement opened we both freaked out.

I looked around for something to use to DEFEND myself, but the best I could come up with was a toilet plunger.

Rowley grabbed a can of lemon dust spray and one of Gramma's handbags. And, when we heard footsteps coming down the stairs, we braced ourselves.

STOMP
STOMP

WORLD'S BEST GRANDMA

The footsteps PAUSED when they got near the bottom, and that's when we made our MOVE.

It turned out it wasn't Mrs McNeil, and it wasn't a BURGLAR, either. It was MOM.

She was there to do a load of laundry, since our washing machine at home is broken.

Mom didn't say much. She just told us to get our winter clothes back on and to get in the car. And she was totally silent on the drive back to our neighbourhood, which was really AWKWARD.

I figured that, as soon as Rowley was out of the car, Mom was gonna yell at me for being at Gramma's house without permission. But she didn't say ANYTHING, and she didn't mention it to Dad during dinner, either.

After I finished doing the dishes, Mom told me she wanted to have a talk in my room. She said it was "perfectly normal" for boys my age to play "make believe", and that there was nothing to feel ashamed of. Then she said she was glad me and Rowley were using our imaginations instead of playing video games.

I have no IDEA what Mom thought we were doing in Gramma's basement. But, to be honest with you, I kind of wish she had just GROUNDED me instead.

<u>Wednesday</u>

It's been snowing for the past few days, and last night we got another inch and a half. Unfortunately, that wasn't enough to close the school, and even if it snowed MORE than that I don't think they would've given us the day off.

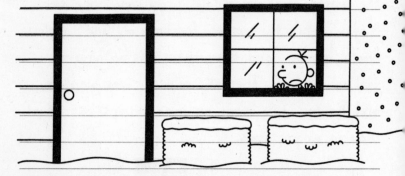

We only get a certain amount of snow days each year and, if we use them all, then we have to make up for them during the summer holidays. And we've already burned through most of our snow days for this winter, even though SOME of them technically weren't used because of SNOW.

In December the school shut down for three days because of a LICE epidemic.

What happened was that Lily Bodner came to school with head lice, but I guess she didn't know. And they SPREAD when she took pictures with her friends.

So, if we're sitting in a hot classroom in July, I guess we can all thank Lily for taking selfies.

Sometimes, when it snows in the morning, they'll give us a HALF-day. But I'm not a big fan of half-days, because we still have to walk all that way just to put in a few hours at school.

What REALLY stinks is when the school looks at the weather forecast and decides in advance that the NEXT day is gonna be a half-day.

On a half-day the school schedule is the same, but everything takes half the time. That goes for DETENTION, too. And all the bullies in our school know that if they do something bad the day BEFORE a half-day they'll only get half the PUNISHMENT.

TRIP

Sometimes school gets cancelled because it's SUPPOSED to snow, and then it DOESN'T. That's because the school relies on our local TV weatherman for the forecast, and he's wrong at least 50% of the time.

GARY GOOFS
AGAIN!

On New Year's Eve he said it was gonna be "T-shirts and shorts weather" the next day, but then it snowed three inches. And when people saw him at the grocery store they let him know they weren't happy.

Honestly, I don't see how this guy still has a JOB. But I guess, as long as people like my parents tune in every night, he's not going ANYWHERE.

I couldn't find one of my gloves this morning, so I looked for a replacement. I was already running late, so the best I could come up with was a puppet Mom bought to try and get me to eat healthy food when I was younger.

I guess Mom thought that if Mr Morsels liked vegetables, then I would, too. But I used Mr Morsels to eat MY vegetables, and when I found him today in the cupboard he still had stains on his face from the peas I wouldn't touch in second grade.

I know it's kind of ridiculous to wear a puppet as a glove, and I MOSTLY remembered to keep that thing tucked in my coat pocket on the walk to school.

But when Cassie Drench rode by in her mom's car I TOTALLY forgot Mr Morsels was still on my hand.

HIIII!

Speaking of GIRLS, there's been a BIG change to the Safety Patrols in the past few weeks.

There used to be a lot of BOYS on the Patrols, but most of them quit or got kicked off before the start of the new year.

The last two boys on the Patrols were Eric Reynolds and Dougie Finch, who were both captains. But they had their badges taken away in the first week of January when they got into a snowball fight in front of the kindergarten classroom at the elementary school.

So now the Safety Patrols are 100% GIRLS. And I'll bet they've been planning a takeover for a WHILE.

The reason is because the guys at my school can be real JERKS. And when it snows they're REALLY bad.

After a while, I'm sure the girls got SICK of it, and that's why they put themselves in charge.

Now that the girls are in power, they're not messing around. If you throw a single snowball on a school day, the Safety Patrols will report you to the principal, and it'll get you an automatic suspension.

So the girls are just PRAYING one of us guys will step out of line.

Today the road was cleared, but the pavement WASN'T. Whenever that happens, me and Rowley just walk in the road. But these new Safety Patrols are sticklers for the rules, and they won't let us walk in the road, even though THEY do it.

But it's practically IMPOSSIBLE to walk on the pavement when it hasn't been ploughed, ESPECIALLY when people are clearing their driveways.

In fact, it's hard to even know where the pavement IS, and this morning I almost busted a kneecap on a fire hydrant that was buried in a snowdrift.

The thing that REALLY stinks is that the Safety Patrols make all us guys walk on the PAVEMENT, but they let all the GIRLS walk on the ROAD.

When me and Rowley got to school today, we were totally wiped out from the trip in. But the girls in our class were fresh and ready to go. And if one of them goes on to be president it's because they got an unfair advantage back in middle school.

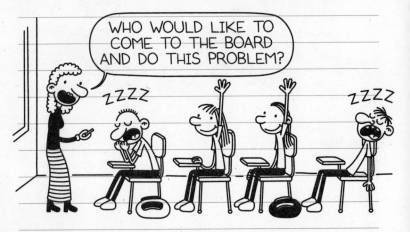

I don't really blame the Safety Patrols for sticking it to the guys in my grade. Most boys are basically SAVAGES, and they make civilized guys like ME look bad.

But, with this new Safety Patrol situation, I've been thinking there might be a way for me to separate myself from those fools.

If I can work FOR the Safety Patrols, I can stay on their GOOD side. And if I report the troublemakers to the girls, then they'll OWE me.

For some reason, though, snitching is really frowned on in my school. If you tell on a kid for doing something WRONG, then everyone says you're a tattletale, and it's hard to recover from that.

But, from what I can tell, the only people the "no snitching" thing helps are the BULLIES. I'm sure they're the ones who came up with the idea in the FIRST place.

Personally, I don't have ANY problem with snitching. And apparently you can make MONEY from being a tattletale.

Rodrick told me about a guy in his high school who turned out to be a "narc", which means the guy PRETENDED to be a high-schooler but was actually a cop in DISGUISE.

I've heard about this kind of thing before, and sometimes I wonder if there are narcs in MIDDLE school, too.

There's a new kid named Shane Browning who came to our school in the middle of the year, and he looks a lot older than the rest of us. I'm starting to wonder if maybe HE'S a narc.

So I've been giving him the inside scoop on my classmates, just in case he is.

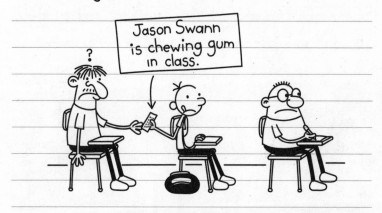

Anyway, the snow situation is causing a LOT of problems. For the past few days kids have been wearing their boots in school, and everyone tracks snow through the hallways.

So today the teachers made everyone take off their boots in the entryway. But the snow on the boots MELTED and made a giant PUDDLE.

Then kids WALKED through the puddle on their way to class, and before long everyone's socks were SOAKED. One thing led to another, and by third period it was just complete CHAOS in the hallways.

It got so bad the teachers had to collect all our socks and keep them in the front office.

But a bunch of barefoot middle-schoolers isn't such a great thing, either.

At the end of the day we all went to the front office to get our socks. But most socks look the SAME, so no one could tell which ones belonged to who.

Luckily, Jake McGough has a really good sense of smell, and he paired each kid up with their correct socks.

He even got the socks right for the Garza twins, which you have to admit is pretty IMPRESSIVE.

I was glad it was a little warmer on the way home today, since me and Rowley didn't have Gramma's house to use as a pit stop. But that didn't mean the walk home was EASY.

You're not allowed to throw snowballs on the way home from school. But AFTER you get home you can do anything you WANT.

So kids who live close to school have figured out that, if they drop their bag off at their house, it counts as being HOME. Then they come after the kids like me and Rowley who still have a long way to WALK.

The SAFETY PATROLS get ambushed, too. But rules are rules, and they're not allowed to fight BACK.

And they get attacked from both SIDES. Some of the kids on my hill who get lifts home walk halfway back to school just to get their licks in.

It's supposed to snow another few inches tomorrow.
I told my parents that I'm saving up for a
SNOWMOBILE so getting to school isn't such a
hassle on days like today.

But Mom and Dad started listing all the reasons
why a middle-school kid can't have a snowmobile,
and after a while I kind of tuned them out.

Any time I come up with a good idea my parents
shoot it down. They did the exact same thing
when I had my dog-sled idea LAST winter.

I figured if I bought a few dogs and trained
them to pull a sled, getting to school in the
morning would be a SNAP.

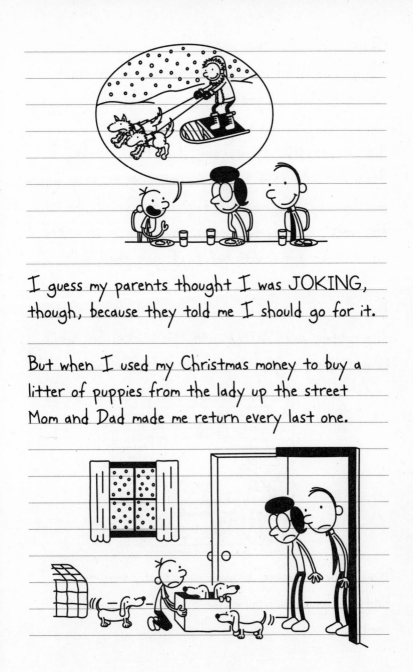

I guess my parents thought I was JOKING, though, because they told me I should go for it.

But when I used my Christmas money to buy a litter of puppies from the lady up the street Mom and Dad made me return every last one.

<u>Thursday</u>
Today reminded me why the winter is my least favourite time of year.

It was another snowy day, but this morning I decided to do some extra preparation to stay warm on the way to school. Dad lit a fire before he left for work, and I figured I could use it to warm up my coat and boots before I put them on.

But I left my boots too close to the fire, and the rubber soles melted into the bricks. So, when it was time to go, they wouldn't BUDGE.

Rowley was coming to get me at any minute, so I had to figure out something ELSE to wear on my feet.

I knew the Safety Patrols wouldn't let us walk in the road, and my sneakers were gonna get SOAKED if I had to walk through the snow.

So I created my own SNOWSHOES out of pizza boxes and duct tape. And by the time Rowley knocked on the door I was ready to go.

I've gotta say, my snowshoes worked even better than I EXPECTED. In fact, I was moving along so fast that Rowley had trouble keeping up with me.

SKISH   SKOOSH

But, once we got to the bottom of Surrey
Street, things fell apart.

The boxes got SOGGY, and I started sinking
into the snow. And then it was even WORSE
than having sneakers on, because now I was
dragging these wet BOXES along with me.

SPLURK SPLURK

I knew this wasn't working, so I had Rowley try
to help me pull the boxes off my sneakers. But it
was practically IMPOSSIBLE, because they were
double-wrapped in duct tape.

CHEW GNAW

Unfortunately, we were right at the edge of the Guzmans' yard, and they've got about eleven dogs. The dogs were curious about what we were doing, and that wasn't helping things.

Then the dogs got AGGRESSIVE and started fighting over the pizza boxes. That's when I remembered there were a few slices of pizza still in them.

The dogs chewed up the pizza boxes and thankfully didn't take off my FEET. We got out of there as quick as we could, but my sneakers were getting soaked in the snow.

The second I stepped onto the road, though, the Safety Patrols were right there with their whistles. So I had to just suck it up and walk on the pavement.

It didn't take long for the COLD to set in. I was worried I could lose my TOES if I didn't find a way to warm them up. But the school was still a long way off, and I was desperate.

So we stopped every few houses, and I'd shove
my feet into a heat vent until I got the feeling
back in my toes.

We finally made it to school. But it took me a
minute to realize it was almost as cold in THERE
as it was OUTSIDE.

Apparently what happened was that the sock
smell from yesterday was so strong that it was
too much for the night janitor.

So he went around and opened all the windows to let some fresh air circulate.

But then I guess he forgot to CLOSE the windows at the end of his shift. And the furnace couldn't keep up, so it shut down. That meant we had a whole day of school with NO HEAT.

At first the teachers let us wear our winter stuff in class. But I guess that was too weird, so they changed their minds and made us put our gear in the lockers.

In History we were FREEZING, but our teacher was just FINE. Mrs Willey keeps an electric heater next to her desk, and she had that thing cranked up to the MAX.

Halfway through class, a girl named Becky Cosgrove tipped her desk over and started yelling, which was totally random.

As punishment, Mrs Willey made Becky sit on a chair next to her desk. And it took a minute for the REST of us to figure out what Becky's game was.

But kids in middle school are idiots, and within thirty seconds EVERYONE was trying to get a seat next to Mrs Willey.

For the rest of the day everybody did whatever they could to keep WARM. And some kids got pretty CREATIVE about it.

We had a school play a few weeks ago, and somebody had the bright idea of getting one of the costumes from behind the stage.

While most of us were freezing our butts off INSIDE, the snow was really piling up OUTSIDE. And by fourth period people were freaking out that we were gonna be stuck at school OVERNIGHT.

At lunch kids bought up everything in the cafeteria so they'd have something to eat if we got snowed in. That sent everyone ELSE into a panic, so kids made a run on the vending machines in the hallways.

At that point people were just trying to get their hands on anything that was EDIBLE. A rumour spread that there was food in the SCIENCE lab, so a bunch of kids ran down THERE.

And, from what I heard, they picked that place
CLEAN.

I think the principal could see that she was about
to have a RIOT on her hands, so she announced
an early hometime.

Well, that was great news for everyone who took
the BUS home, but us kids who had to WALK
didn't have it so easy. I really wasn't looking
forward to walking home in a snowstorm, so I
came up with an IDEA. Whirley Street isn't too
far from OUR neighbourhood, so I figured me
and Rowley could take THEIR bus and then
WALK the rest of the way.

So, after we got out of school, we headed straight for the bus line. And we were so bundled up that nobody even NOTICED when we got on board.

I've gotta say, it was kind of WEIRD being on the bus with the Whirley Street kids, because those guys are our ENEMIES. They used to sledge on our hill every winter until they discovered the 13th hole at the golf course.

The 13th hole is LEGENDARY, and everyone knows it's the best sledging hill in our town. But the problem is that the golf course is part of the country club, so if you sledge there you're TRESPASSING.

Last year I wanted to see what the fuss over the 13th hole was all about, so I got Rowley to come with me. But Rowley was SUPER nervous about the trespassing thing, so he didn't want to go.

I had to remind Rowley that he and his family are MEMBERS of the country club, so technically he WOULDN'T be trespassing.

But I guess Rowley was worried his family might lose their membership if he got caught sledging. So, to disguise himself, he shook his face really fast and kept that up the whole time we were there.

SHAKE
SHAKE

I've gotta admit, the 13th hole was everything people SAID it was.

It was really STEEP, and someone built up a mound of snow near the bottom where kids were catching some SERIOUS air.

We got in a few good runs, but that's when the WHIRLEY Street kids came and kicked everyone ELSE off the golf course so they could have it to THEMSELVES.

But I was OK with that. As long as those guys aren't causing trouble on OUR street, they can have the whole GOLF COURSE for all I care.

The bus ride with the Whirley Street kids wasn't a lot of fun, but me and Rowley just tried to keep a low profile so no one would notice us.

We were almost at Whirley Street when one of the kids at the back did something really DUMB. Some fool actually threw a snowball ON THE BUS.

ZIP

SPLAT

The second it happened the driver pulled over. She said she wasn't moving until the person who threw the snowball turned themself in.

Like I said before, there's a "no snitching" rule in middle school, so no one from the back of the bus made a PEEP. I wish I knew who did it, because I would've given them up in a HEARTBEAT.

I was pretty sure the bus driver was just BLUFFING about not moving, and that we'd be on our way within a few minutes.

But then she broke out a BOOK and started on page ONE. So we just sat there and waited for an HOUR while she read.

The worst part about the whole thing was that the bus driver turned off the ENGINE, so there was no HEAT.

There was some conversation going on at the back of the bus, and I think a few kids were trying to get the one who threw the snowball to give himself up.

But I really wish I hadn't turned round to look, because, when I DID, some eighth-grader realized I wasn't from Whirley Street.

That was all it took. These guys needed someone to take the BLAME for the snowball, and since I was an OUTSIDER it was a no-brainer for them.

The bus driver said I needed to get off the bus IMMEDIATELY. That was fine with ME, because now that my cover was blown I didn't wanna stick around any longer than I HAD to. So I got off the bus, and Rowley was two steps behind me.

VROOM

I was pretty sure we were about a mile from Surrey Street. The street we were on didn't have pavements, and there weren't any Safety Patrols this far out, so we walked on the road.

Five minutes later we heard angry voices. It was a bunch of Whirley Street kids, and they were coming straight FOR us.

First, those idiots LIED about me throwing the snowball on the bus. Then they BELIEVED their lie, and now they were MAD.

Me and Rowley had to make a choice. We could either deal with the mob or RUN. We decided to run, and the only place to go was into the WOODS.

Believe me, that was the LAST thing I wanted to do. Everyone knows the woods along that road are where the GOAT MAN lives, which is why nobody ever goes in there.

Rodrick was the first one to tell me about the Goat Man, who he said was half man, half goat.

I wasn't sure if he meant the top half was a GOAT and the bottom part was a MAN, or if it was the other way round. But, either way, the Goat Man seemed pretty scary to ME.

Me and Rowley have argued for YEARS over which version is right. Rowley thinks the Goat Man is split down the MIDDLE.

I guess Rowley could be RIGHT, but, if you ask me, I think his version sounds kind of STUPID.

It's fun talking about this stuff when we're on a sleepover and safe in our sleeping bags. But, now that we were in the woods where the Goat Man actually LIVES, it was no laughing matter.

The Whirley Street kids must've known about the Goat Man, too, because when we went into the woods they didn't follow us. I figured we'd stay in there just long enough for the Whirley Street kids to LEAVE, because we didn't want to be in there any longer than we HAD to.

But those guys must've known we were too chicken to stay in there for long, and we could see them waiting for us on the road at the edge of the woods.

So our only choice was to go deeper in, and that's what we did.

What was WEIRD was how QUIET it was in there. After a while, I realized we couldn't hear the cars on the road, and that's when I knew we'd gone in TOO deep.

We followed our footsteps back to the road, but the sun was going down, and it was getting hard to find our tracks.

We picked up the pace because we didn't wanna get stuck in the woods in the DARK. But when we came across a set of tracks we FROZE.

At first we thought it was the GOAT MAN. But then we realized there were TWO sets of footprints, and they were OURS. That meant we'd spent the past ten minutes walking in a giant CIRCLE.

So we turned round and headed in the OTHER direction. But then we ran into a CREEK, and I knew we were lost.

GURGLE GURGLE

Rowley was PANICKING, but I wasn't. I knew that, if you get lost in the wilderness, as long as you have WATER you're FINE.

I saw a movie where these explorers got trapped in the mountains, but they found a spring and it kept them alive.

But then I remembered that when they got DESPERATE they had to eat their pack animals. I just hoped things didn't reach that point for US.

I figured, if we followed the creek, it might LEAD us somewhere, and at least we wouldn't get lost again. But, when we came across a beaver dam, Rowley started freaking out.

Rowley said that beavers are DANGEROUS, and that he saw a show on TV where a beaver attacked a PERSON.

But Rowley's an idiot. The show he was talking about was a CARTOON, and I was actually WITH him when he watched it.

Still, I couldn't convince Rowley to stay near the creek, so we had to turn round AGAIN. And by now it was REALLY dark. After walking a few more minutes, something bright caught my eye. I thought maybe it was the headlights from a car, and we ran towards it.

It turned out the light WAS coming from a car, but it was just a rusty piece of junk in the middle of the woods. And what caught my eye was the reflection of the MOON on the bumper.

When my eyes adjusted to the light, I realized there were a LOT of abandoned cars and trucks all around us.

I saw something shiny sitting on a stump and I picked it up. The thing was cold and metal, and when I held it up to my face to take a closer look I knew EXACTLY what it was.

It was a BELT BUCKLE, and it belonged to MECKLEY MINGO.

That meant me and Rowley were smack in the middle of the Mingos' CAMP.

People in my town have always wondered where the Mingos live, and now me and Rowley had stumbled into their HEADQUARTERS.

I thought we were LUCKY, because at least there was no one THERE. But, when I turned to LEAVE, something grabbed my HAND.

Well, technically, something grabbed Mr Morsels. I thought for SURE it was Meckley Mingo and he was gonna KILL me for touching his belt buckle.

Thankfully, I was WRONG. The puppet was snagged on a truck's door handle, so I tried to pull it free.

That's when we heard noises coming from INSIDE THE TRUCK. I realized I had to choose between saving MYSELF and saving a PUPPET, and it was no contest.

Me and Rowley tore out of there. But when we were a good distance away from the Mingos' camp we heard a sound that made my blood run cold.

I didn't know if it was the GOAT MAN or the MINGO KIDS.

All I knew for sure was that if we stopped
RUNNING we'd be DEAD.

I could hear shouting behind us, and it was
getting CLOSER. But, just when it felt like the
voices were right on TOP of us, we broke through
the trees and into the open.

Luckily, Dad was paying ATTENTION, or me
and Rowley would've been ROADKILL.

But at least it would've been over QUICK. Because
if the MINGOS had caught us I'm sure they
would've taken their TIME.

Friday

When I woke up this morning, I was totally EXHAUSTED. My legs felt like rubber from all that running yesterday, and I barely got any rest because I had a nightmare the Mingos were chasing me.

I was gonna tell Mom I couldn't go to school today, but when I looked out of the window I realized I didn't HAVE to.

It had snowed at least five inches overnight, which meant school was CLOSED. So I was looking forward to a nice, relaxing day of doing absolutely NOTHING.

Mom and Dad were already gone, and Manny was at nursery. Rodrick usually sleeps past 1:00 p.m. on snow days, so I more or less had the whole house to MYSELF.

I went downstairs to get a bowl of cereal and turn on the TV. But there was something wrong with the REMOTE.

PRESS
PRESS

I noticed it felt a little LIGHT, so I opened up the back of the remote to see if there was a missing battery.

It turns out there weren't ANY batteries inside, but there was a note from MOM.

To get the batteries
for the remote,
load the dishwasher.

I really didn't feel like doing chores on a SNOW DAY, so I looked around the house for some batteries I could put in the remote. But Mom must've KNOWN I'd do that because there wasn't a spare battery ANYWHERE.

JIGGLE
JIGGLE

I couldn't figure out how Mom was gonna know I'd loaded the dishwasher, since she wasn't even HOME. But when I put in the last plate and shut the door I found something.

It was another NOTE with a BATTERY taped to it.

> Congratulations!
> Clean the downstairs bathroom to get your next battery!

I didn't like where this was heading. The TV remote takes FOUR batteries, and at this rate I was gonna burn through my whole DAY doing chores.

But then I realized I didn't HAVE to. The remote in Mom and Dad's bedroom is really SKINNY, and I was pretty sure it only took ONE battery.

And it turned out I was RIGHT. I knew I was
gonna have to finish all the chores before Mom
and Dad got home, but I figured I had plenty
of time and I deserved to enjoy myself for a
little while. So I made myself comfortable on their
bed and turned on the TV.

Ordinarily I get a little weirded out being in
Mom and Dad's bed, but today I decided to make
an exception. ESPECIALLY when I realized one
of their blankets was the one we got from Aunt
Dorothy for Christmas.

Watching TV in bed was AWESOME, or at least
for a WHILE. I was comfortable for the FIRST
two hours, but after that my neck started
hurting from lying in that position.

I've already decided that when I get a place of my own I'm gonna attach my TV to the CEILING so I can look straight UP at it. But I'm gonna get someone who knows what they're DOING to install the TV, because I don't need to be the next Flat Stanley.

I must've dozed off for a while, because when the phone rang it startled me. It was MOM, and I figured she was checking up on me to see if I'd finished my chores.

But the reason she was calling was to tell me she couldn't make it home in time to pick Manny up from nursery, so she was gonna have Mrs Drummond drop Manny off at the HOUSE.

That meant I had to BABYSIT, which was gonna really mess up the rest of my day.

When Mrs Drummond dropped Manny off half an hour later, I didn't know what to DO with him. I put him in Mom and Dad's room and turned on some cartoons, but he followed me back downstairs. So I guess Manny just wanted to be with ME.

I tried to remember what Rodrick used to do with me when I was little. But all I could think of was the time he gave me lemon juice and told me it was SODA.

Then I remembered a game me and Rodrick used to play that was actually FUN. We pretended the floor was LAVA, and we had to stay OFF it by using cushions from the couch.

Me and Rodrick used to play that game for HOURS. I figured, if I got Manny started, he could keep himself entertained while I wrapped up my chores. But when I told Manny how the game WORKED he totally freaked out.

So now Manny wouldn't go anywhere near the FLOOR. And that made things really inconvenient for me.

But I still had to do my chores, or I'd be in trouble when Mom and Dad got home. And I had a BIG one in front of me, which was clearing the driveway.

I knew Manny would have a total meltdown if I left him inside with all that lava, so I got him dressed in his snow gear, which wasn't easy.

I figured Manny could play on the back decking while I shovelled the driveway, and he'd be safe because the decking is closed in.

The snow on the driveway was wet and heavy, and it was hard to make any progress. After a half-hour, I decided to take a break and soak my hands in some warm water.

While I was inside, I figured I'd check and see how Manny was doing out on the back decking. But Manny was GONE. He had built a little staircase out of snow to escape.

Thankfully, he didn't get FAR. But I realized I couldn't leave him ALONE any more.

I took Manny to the front yard with me. It was getting late, and Dad gets REALLY mad when the driveway's not cleared when he comes home from work.

So I shovelled as fast as I could, and Manny pitched in to help.

But there was just too much snow, and not enough TIME. I was ready to give up when some girls from a different neighbourhood walked by and offered to clear our driveway for ten bucks.

These kids looked YOUNG, and I didn't see how they could do any better than me and Manny. But we could use all the help we could get, so I was willing to give them a CHANCE.

I had five dollars in the drawer next to my bed, and I got the other five from the big jar of change Manny has in his room. But what I didn't realize when I agreed to the deal with those girls was that they had a SNOWBLOWER.

So they were done clearing the whole driveway within five minutes.

I felt like I was getting ripped off, so I told them I'd pay them three bucks instead of ten.

But I guess this wasn't the FIRST time someone had tried to stiff them on payment. They moved all the snow BACK onto the driveway and added the snow from the front lawn just to make a point.

By the time my PARENTS got home, things
were worse than when I STARTED.

After dinner Mom and Dad lectured me until
about eight o'clock for not finishing my chores.
And that's when Rodrick got out of bed to
start his day.

<u>Saturday</u>
I usually sleep IN at weekends, but this morning
Mom had OTHER plans for me.

She said I was going to spend the whole day
OUTSIDE. I told her I'd go out in the snow
after I'd played some video games, but she
reminded me about Screen-Free Weekends, and I
knew she wasn't gonna budge.

When I was younger, I could spend HOURS
playing in the snow. But, nowadays, after about
ten minutes I'm ready to come inside.

Grown-ups act like being in the snow is the most
fun you can ever have. But you never see THEM
out there rolling around in it.

I can only remember one time Dad played with us out in the snow. But THAT ended the second Rodrick dumped snow down the back of Dad's NECK.

SLORP

Mom's ALWAYS making us kids go outside because she says we need our vitamin D, which you get from the sun. I tell Mom I get PLENTY of vitamin D from the sun in my video games, but that kind of reasoning never works on her.

When I went outside today, Manny was
already in the front yard making snowmen, or
WHATEVER you'd call those things.

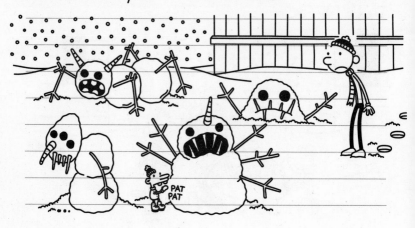

We never finished raking the lawn in the autumn,
so Manny used the leaves we hadn't picked up to
decorate his snow friends.

Manny had used up most of the snow in the yard,
so there wasn't a whole lot I could even DO
outside. I decided to head up to Rowley's, which
meant I had to pass by FREGLEY'S house.
And, sure enough, he was out in his front yard.

WANNA FINISH
"BUILDING" ME?

The reason I went to Rowley's was because his family
just got heated floors. So on cold days I try to
spend as much time at his house as POSSIBLE.

AHHHH...

But Mom must've KNOWN I was gonna go to Rowley's because she called his parents and he was outside when I got there.

As long as we both had to be outdoors, I figured we should make the most of it. Since I'd already done all the hard work getting up the hill, I told Rowley we should get in a little sledging.

The plough usually comes through by late morning, so we can only get in a few good runs before the street is cleared. But the regular plough guy was on HOLIDAY, and the kids at the top of the hill told the SUBSTITUTE driver that Surrey Street was two miles down the road. So that bought us some extra time.

I don't actually think it's a good idea to mess around with substitutes because it ALWAYS comes back to bite you. Last year we had a long-term supply teacher in Algebra, and on his first day me and my classmates all switched seats with each other because we knew the sub would be relying on the seating chart.

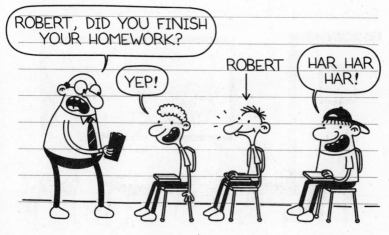

ROBERT, DID YOU FINISH YOUR HOMEWORK?

YEP!

ROBERT

HAR HAR HAR!

I've gotta say, it was pretty hilarious having him call us by the wrong names every day. But when the kid pretending to be ME started acting like a total JERK it wasn't so funny any more.

GREG HEFFLEY, YOU COME DOWN RIGHT THIS INSTANT!

And when our REAL teacher got back the sub gave her a write-up on the FAKE Greg Heffley, which landed ME in detention for two weeks.

Rowley only has one sledge, but there's just enough room on it for two people. We squeezed aboard and pointed it down the hill, but with all that weight we couldn't really get any momentum.

When we got close to the bottom of the hill, we came to a dead stop. But that was probably a GOOD thing because the kids who made it all the way down got nailed by the Lower Surrey Street kids when they crossed into their territory.

Things could've got a lot uglier, but then the substitute snowplough driver worked out where Surrey Street was, and that was the end of THAT.

By then I figured we had been outside long enough, and we tried to go inside. But Mom had locked the door, and I could tell she wasn't messing around.

Since we couldn't SLEDGE any more, we needed to find something ELSE to do. So me and Rowley went to the empty lot a few doors up from my house to decide what to do NEXT.

I figured that as long as we had to be outside we might as well stay WARM. At school we watched a movie about people in the Arctic who build IGLOOS to survive in the cold weather, and I thought maybe we could give it a try.

We made some snow bricks and stacked them the way the people in the movie did. It was hard at first, but then we started getting the HANG of it. The main thing was getting the shape of the dome just right so it didn't COLLAPSE.

We were really careful, and everything held together. But when we put in the last brick at the top we realized we forgot to build a DOOR.

Rowley started hyperventilating, and I knew if I didn't DO something he was gonna suck up all the oxygen in there. So I busted through the top and took a big gulp of fresh air.

GASP!

Some neighbourhood kids had been watching us build our igloo and, with my head sticking up, I must've looked like an easy target.

160

After those idiots ran out of snowballs, they
climbed on top of the igloo. But it wasn't meant
to support any weight, and within a few seconds
the whole thing came crashing down.

Me and Rowley were lucky to crawl out of there
ALIVE. Once we pulled ourselves out of our ruined
igloo, I decided that we'd had enough fun for one
day. So we went back to the house, and this time
Mom let us IN.

I told Mom what happened at the empty lot and
how she needed to go out there and yell at those
stupid kids for us.

But Mom said that learning to deal with "conflict"
is part of growing up, and that me and Rowley
were gonna have to deal with this on our OWN.
I didn't like the sound of THAT. I thought the
whole POINT of having parents is that you've
got someone to solve your problems FOR you.

Dad was listening from the other room, and he
had a TOTALLY different take. He said that
the neighbourhood kids had just declared WAR
on me and Rowley, and if we didn't fight BACK
they'd think it was OK to attack us whenever
they WANTED.

Dad said that when HE was growing up his neighbourhood turned into a BATTLEFIELD every time it snowed. Kids built giant snow forts and had epic snowball fights, and everyone was part of a different "clan".

Dad said each clan had its own FLAG, and when you captured somebody else's fort you planted a flag to mark your territory.

Well, Rowley thought WE should form a clan, and he really liked this FLAG idea. I thought it seemed kind of DUMB, but as long as making a flag gave us an excuse to be INDOORS for a while I was all for it.

We found an old pillowcase in the laundry room and got some markers out of the junk drawer in the kitchen. We started by trying to come up with a NAME for our clan.

Rowley said he wanted us to be "Hufflepuff", but I said if we were gonna do this I wanted our name to be something ORIGINAL.

We argued back and forth for a while about our name, and I realized we weren't gonna agree on one. So we talked about how our flag should LOOK.

Rowley wanted our symbol to be a WOLF, but I wanted something even fiercer than THAT, so we'd scare kids off. I thought a bloody battle-axe would do the trick, but of course Rowley didn't like that idea. So we compromised and put the two things TOGETHER.

But when you add an axe and a wolf you just get a dead wolf, which isn't gonna scare ANYONE.

We were going to start over and make a new flag, but when I got another pillowcase Mom told us we needed to go back outside. So we put on our snow gear and went to the empty lot.

The kids who wrecked our igloo had moved on to other things, so me and Rowley had the empty lot all to ourselves. We used the snow from the igloo as a starting point and made a fort that could hold up to an attack.

After we were finished, we planted our flag on top of the wall and WAITED.

I figured our fort might attract some attention, but I didn't realize just how MUCH. Within a few minutes we had kids coming at us from every DIRECTION.

We were COMPLETELY outgunned, and when the kids rushed our fort we had to ABANDON it.

When we got back to the house, we told Dad what happened. But, after we described our fort to him, he said we'd done everything all WRONG.

He said we needed to build our fort on HIGH ground so we could drive back our enemies.

Then Dad launched into a big history lesson on castle warfare and all the things that people did to defend themselves back in medieval times.

The stuff they did in the old days was totally BRUTAL, and here's just one example. When invaders tried to climb the walls of a castle, the people inside would pour boiling OIL on them.

I hope it doesn't get to that level in our neighbourhood battles. But tonight I added an item to Mom's grocery list just in case it DOES.

Shopping List	
Eggs	Peas
Milk	Pears
Ketchup	Batteries
Bread	
Pickles	OIL

<u>Sunday</u>

It must've snowed another seven inches last
night, and the street was totally COVERED
when I woke up. I couldn't even see the line
between our YARD and the ROAD.

I was kind of surprised the plough hadn't come
yet because when there's THIS much snow people
can't even get their cars out of their driveways.
But when Dad came back from his morning walk I
found out what was going on.

Dad said that when the plough tried to get up the hill it had got STUCK. And when the snowplough driver was ambushed by the neighbourhood kids he ran off and left the truck sitting in the street.

That meant we could sledge all DAY if we wanted to. But sledging is for KIDS, and I had OTHER plans in mind.

I'd been up all night looking through Dad's books to learn everything I could about castle warfare and battle strategies. And by the morning I was READY.

I wanted to get started making a fort with Rowley right away, but I knew that the second we put up WALLS we were gonna be under ATTACK. The only way we could fight back was if we had AMMUNITION.

I figured we could buy a big supply of pre-made snowballs from Mitchell Pickett, so we went down to his shed, which was open for business. But I guess things must've gone well for Mitchell last winter because THIS year he EXPANDED his operations.

I'd borrowed enough money from Manny's change jar to pay for three dozen snowballs, but now that I saw all this OTHER stuff I had to make some tough choices.

The Sloppy Specials looked like regular snowballs
to me, so I asked Mitchell why they were five
times more expensive. He said that each one was
a regular snowball with SLUSH inside, and don't
even ask me how he pulled THAT off.

We ended up buying two dozen pre-made snowballs
and one snowball launcher, which I figured we could
use if we needed to nail somebody from long distance.

But I wish I'd brought the whole jar of change
because Mitchell was selling a snow catapult that
looked like it could REALLY do some damage.

I'd have to get that another time, though. We
loaded up my sledge with our purchases and went
back to the empty lot.

But when we got closer we were SHOCKED by
what we saw. There were a BUNCH of snow
forts in the lot now, and there were kids inside
each one.

These kids had copied our idea, right down to the
FLAGS. The Marlee sisters had a spear on their
flag, and Evelyn Trimble had a bat on hers. The
Garza twins had a two-headed ogre, which actually
looked pretty cool.

There were some really LAME flags, too. Marcus Marconi's dad owned the sandwich shop in the centre of town that had gone out of business, and Marcus used the flag that used to hang in front of the shop.

I wanted to get closer to see who ELSE had made a fort, but when we got near the lot Ernesto, Gabriel and a bunch of OTHER kids opened FIRE on us.

The lot was totally overcrowded, and I knew there was no WAY we could build a snow fort there. So our only chance was to take over someone ELSE'S.

I got some old binoculars from my garage so we could scope things out without having to get too CLOSE.

Things had got a lot CRAZIER in the five minutes we were gone, though. Gabriel and Ernesto were in a battle with the Marlee sisters, and a bunch of home-schooled kids were going at it with the Garza twins.

Emilia Greenwall and Evelyn Trimble had teamed up to fight Anthony Denard and Sheldon Reyes, and Speed Bump and Latricia Hooks were actually going at it with their FISTS.

But I wasn't focused on all that. I was searching for a fort that looked VULNERABLE, and I FOUND one. The duplex kids had built a pretty solid-looking fort, but as usual it looked like they weren't getting along.

I figured they'd wear themselves out fighting, and when they DID me and Rowley could POUNCE. So we moved in a little closer and waited for the right moment.

That's when I noticed a fort that didn't have anyone IN it. The fort was sitting all alone on top of a big mound of snow. I remembered what Dad said about the HIGH ground, and this fort was in the PERFECT spot.

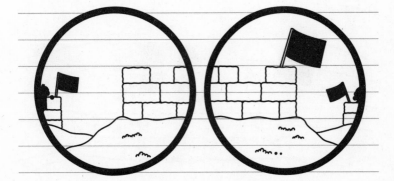

I couldn't figure out why someone would build a fort and ABANDON it, but I knew this was our big chance. So we sneaked around it and climbed over the back wall.

It turned out the fort WASN'T empty, though. It belonged to BABY GIBSON, who was inside with a stockpile of snowballs.

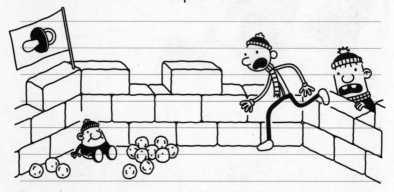

But the second we stepped into the fort it was under ATTACK.

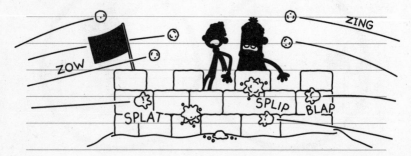

The home-schooled kids must've known about the
high-ground thing, too, and now they wanted
the fort for THEMSELVES. But when they
came charging up the mound we drove them back.
And even Baby Gibson got in on the act.

Then kids started coming for us from every
direction, and it was getting harder and harder
to defend the fort.

The duplex kids split into two groups, and they
came at us from the left AND the right, while
Ernesto and Gabriel started using snowball
throwers to target us from THEIR fort.

And, while we were trying to deal with all THAT, some little kid from Mrs Jimenez's playgroup tunnelled up through the bottom of our fort and TOTALLY took us off guard.

The next thing we knew, our fort was totally infested with PRE-SCHOOLERS. And, to cap it all, the Marlee sisters did a sneak attack from the rear, which was terrifying because those girls go for the EYES.

Me and Rowley got driven out of the fort and onto the open battlefield, where it was just total MAYHEM. Everyone was fighting everyone ELSE, and any sense of order was just GONE.

Then something happened that made everyone STOP. Joe O'Rourke got hit in the mouth with an ice ball and lost a couple of TEETH.

In our neighbourhood, ice balls are on the "banned" list in snowball fights. So, when somebody crossed that line, everybody knew things had gone too far.

Representatives from all the clans had a meeting in the centre of the empty lot to settle on the RULES.

Everyone agreed that ice balls were off-limits, and so was yellow snow. We came up with a bunch of OTHER rules, too, like how it's not OK to stuff snow in someone's hat and then put it back on their head.

Once we agreed on everything, we were ready for the next round of battle.

But, while we were doing all that TALKING, we didn't notice what was happening right BEHIND us.

The Lower Surrey Street kids had sneaked up to the top of the hill with their sledges, and by then there was nothing we could do to STOP them.

Now, if there's ONE thing that unites us hill kids, it's when the kids from the BOTTOM of the hill try to take what's OURS. We don't have much, but we have the HILL, and no one's gonna take that from us.

As long as the plough was stuck, we knew those guys were just gonna keep COMING.

So we decided to DO something about it.

The only way to keep the Lower Surrey Street
kids from coming back up the hill was to build a
WALL to block their path. And we didn't wanna
build some puny wall they could just push over,
either. We wanted something that was SOLID.

But we needed to make it FAST because those
guys were already marching back up the hill with
their sledges. So we got recycling bins from some
nearby houses and started BUILDING.

We made it a DOUBLE wall, so if anyone broke
through the first layer they'd still have to deal
with the SECOND one. And we stockpiled a
TON of snowballs.

We weren't gonna be able to get boiling oil, so I sent Rowley up to his house to fill some thermoses with hot chocolate.

The home-schooled kids went out and collected icicles to stick into the wall, and the duplex kids threw together some snowmen to make it seem like there were more of us than there actually WERE.

And when the Lower Surrey Street kids came BACK we were READY for them.

When those guys saw our WALL, they didn't know what to DO.

And when they got CLOSER we hit them with everything we had.

Those guys didn't stand a CHANCE. We sent them running back down the hill, and we celebrated our victory.

But we celebrated too SOON. Ten minutes later the Lower Surrey Street kids were BACK.

And this time they were armed to the TEETH.

MARCH MARCH MARCH

Most of them were wearing sports gear to protect themselves from our snowballs. And the moment I knew this wasn't gonna be an easy fight was when one of them threw a HOCKEY STICK.

THWOK

But still WE were the ones with the WALL, and we had the higher ground.

So we unleashed another round of snowballs.

We held them off for a while, but those guys had some surprises up their sleeves. They hit us with a round of Sloppy Specials, which we were TOTALLY unprepared for.

If the Lower Surrey Street kids had Sloppy Specials, that meant Mitchell Pickett was playing both SIDES.

But we'd have to deal with him LATER because now we had a NEW problem.

It turned out the Sloppy Specials were just a distraction to draw our attention away from the NEXT wave of attack, which was coming at us FAST.

We hit the kids carrying ladders with snowballs, but, before we knew it, they'd planted their ladders at the base of the wall and had started climbing their way UP it.

But Rowley came back with the hot chocolate just in the nick of time.

We emptied the thermoses out on the kids scaling the wall. Unfortunately, Rowley hadn't added any WATER to the hot-chocolate mix, so all it did was ANNOY them.

I thought those guys were about to take control of the wall, but then Latricia Hooks and Speed Bump saved the day by dumping trash cans full of SLUSH on them.

We didn't have a second to celebrate, though, because the Lower Surrey Street kids were already launching their next attack.

Half the fifth-grade football team lives at the bottom of the hill, and they tried to take down the wall with brute FORCE.

But the wall held UP, and those guys wore themselves out with the effort.

By now EVERYONE was tired. The sun was out, and it was actually starting to get WARM. I really wished I hadn't worn my thermal underwear because I was ROASTING with those extra layers.

The Lower Surrey Street kids kept coming at us, and we kept driving them BACK. And after a while NOBODY had the energy to keep fighting.

Finally, the other team turned round and went back home. At first we thought that meant we had WON. But those guys weren't giving up. They were just REFUELLING.

By now it was lunchtime, and the kids at the bottom of the hill came back outside with sandwiches and snacks.

And when some kid started handing out JUICE CARTONS it was a little hard to watch.

We were all pretty thirsty on the wall, and it was only getting HOTTER.

Some kids started sucking on SNOWBALLS to stay hydrated, and they got through half our stockpile before the rest of us realized what was happening.

We took an inventory of what we had left, and we knew we didn't have enough to fight off a major assault. So we split our remaining snowballs into thirds and put Anthony Denard in charge of protecting them.

We kept waiting for the next attack from the Lower Surrey Street kids, but it never came.

After a while, we realized their strategy was to wait us out until we CRACKED and then take our wall without a fight.

Pervis Gentry was the first one on our side to break. He hadn't even had BREAKFAST this morning, so the sight of all those sandwich crusts lying on the ground made him CRAZY.

He climbed over the wall and ran down the hill, and that was the last any of us saw of him.

But the REST of us hill kids kept it together. Three HOURS went by, but the Lower Surrey Street kids weren't BUDGING.

In fact, they looked like they were settling in for the NIGHT.

A few of them had strung extension cords to their houses, so now they had ELECTRICITY. And we could see the glow of their TV sets from where WE were.

Things were going from bad to worse on the wall. A lot of the younger kids were tired and hungry and wanted to go HOME. And I couldn't blame them, because by now it was DINNERTIME.

Jacob Hoff said he was supposed to have a clarinet lesson at six o'clock, and if he missed it his parents would be mad. And the rest of us could understand that kind of thing.

Jacob's house was just a few doors down, and we told him if he made a run for it we'd give him COVER. He promised that the second his clarinet lesson was over he'd come back to the wall with his coat pockets stuffed with granola bars and fruit chews.

That got everybody pretty excited, and we helped Jacob over the wall. Sure enough, as soon as he touched down on the other side, the Lower Surrey Street kids opened fire on him. But we fired BACK and got Jacob to his front door safely.

It turned out it was a wasted effort, though. The thing about the clarinet lesson was just an excuse to go home, and when we saw Jacob at his bedroom window we knew he was never coming back with those SNACKS.

After that, the mood inside the wall was really
GRIM. Some kids were crying, and I didn't see
how we could hold out much longer.

The Lower Surrey Street kids must've known
they had us on the ropes, because that's when
they launched paper aeroplanes into our fort with
NOTES written on them.

SURRENDER NOW
AND YOU CAN
LEAVE UNHARMED.

That was too much for some kids to take. Even
Baby Gibson seemed shaken, so I guess now we
know he can READ.

A few minutes later a kid came running towards
us from between a couple of houses to the right
of our fort, and we got ready to pelt him with a
round of snowballs.

But somebody RECOGNIZED the kid, and we
held our fire. It was TREVOR NIX, who used
to live on the hill.

Trevor was out of breath and could barely get his words out. So we pulled him up over the wall and waited for him to calm down.

After Trevor got himself together, he told us what was going on. He said the Lower Surrey Street kids had been holding him CAPTIVE, but he managed to ESCAPE.

Trevor said those guys were planning something really BAD, and he wanted to tell us before it was too LATE.

He said the Lower Surrey Street kids were creating a HUGE stockpile of snowballs, and when it got dark they were gonna launch a full-scale attack. But that wasn't even the WORST part.

Those guys were making their snowballs in the
GUZMANS' yard, and that's the place with all
the DOGS. So that meant they were using
YELLOW SNOW and who knows what ELSE.

Everyone was pretty mad about what the Lower
Surrey Street kids were planning, but we were glad
Trevor had given us the heads-up. We told him that
from now on he could sledge on our hill ANY time.

We agreed we couldn't just sit there and wait for
the attack, so we started working on a PLAN.
Half of us would sneak down the hill and launch a
SURPRISE attack on the kids making snowballs
in the Guzmans' yard. The OTHER half would
stay back to protect the fort. We sketched the
plan in the snow with a stick to make sure we were
all on the same page.

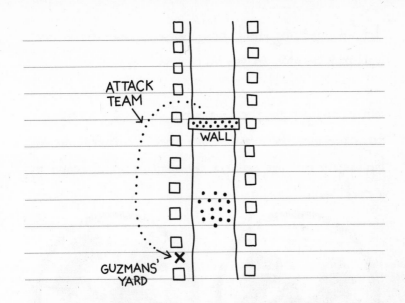

Me and Rowley wanted to be a part of the
ACTION, so we chose to be on the sneak attack
team. Our group loaded up a few sledges with all
the snowballs we had left, and we slipped over the
back wall and between some houses.

It was getting dark now, so we knew those guys wouldn't be able to see us coming.

When we got to the Guzmans' yard, we stopped to scope out the scene. Sure enough, there was a big group of kids making snowballs at the front by a rock wall.

When Baby Gibson gave the signal, we launched our attack.

FLING

But the other guys didn't even FLINCH when we hit them. And as we got closer we realized it was all just a TRICK.

The Lower Surrey Street kids had created DECOYS to split us up, which meant we'd been double-crossed by TREVOR NIX. We rushed back to the wall, but by then it was already too LATE.

The wall was in RUINS, and we were out of ammo. It looked really bad for us hill kids, but then something happened that gave us HOPE.

A group of kids was marching up the hill towards us, and when they got closer I realized it was the SAFETY PATROLS. For a brief second I thought they were there to SAVE us.

But they weren't there to help ANYONE. They were there for REVENGE.

Usually the Safety Patrols aren't allowed to throw snowballs, but today was a SUNDAY. And that meant they were free to do whatever they WANTED.

Half the girls on the Safety Patrols are on the SOFTBALL team, and anybody who says girls can't throw hard doesn't know what they're TALKING about.

The battle turned into the Surrey Street kids versus the Safety Patrols, and we outnumbered them two to one. But then half the girls on our street switched SIDES, and it got really confusing.

In the middle of all this, ANOTHER group came down from the TOP of the hill. It was the WHIRLEY STREET kids, who must've got kicked off the golf course and were coming to sledge on our street. And once THEY got into the mix it was just a total FREE-FOR-ALL.

Just when things couldn't get any CRAZIER,
a terrifying sound cut through the air, and
everyone stopped to figure out what it WAS. The
only ones on the street who knew for SURE were
me and Rowley.

Then the MINGO kids started pouring out of
the woods, looking like they'd just woken up from a
three-month NAP.

The last Mingo to emerge was MECKLEY. He was carrying something on top of a STICK, and at first I couldn't tell what it was. But when he got CLOSER I realized it was MR MORSELS.

Meckley wasn't wearing his BELT, which I thought was strange. But seeing that made me remember something, and I reached into my coat pocket and pulled out something cold and metal.

When me and Rowley were in the Mingos' camp, I must've put the belt buckle in my pocket without even REALIZING it. And now I was in a panic, because that meant Meckley Mingo was coming for ME.

But the only thing kids in my town hate more than each OTHER is the MINGOS. So, when the Mingos charged, everyone turned to FACE them.

Well, everyone except ME. At that point I'd had ENOUGH.

When the Mingos came at us, I looked for a good place to HIDE.

There was a big hole in a collapsed section of the wall, so I dived inside, and Rowley was right behind me. The battle raged all around us, and I didn't see how we were gonna get out of this one ALIVE.

Rowley didn't think we were gonna make it, either. He told me that if I survived but he DIDN'T I could have all of his video games.

I patted myself down to see if I had a pen so he could put that in WRITING, but all I had on me was that stupid belt buckle.

It didn't matter anyway, because five seconds later the ground started shaking, and it felt like we were in an EARTHQUAKE.

I thought we were gonna be buried ALIVE, and all I could think of is how the two of us were gonna end up in a MUSEUM after they dug us out in a couple of thousand years.

But then the ground stopped shaking, and after a few seconds we popped our heads out of our hiding spot to see what was happening.

The snowplough was three quarters of the way up the street, mowing through everything in its path. And I don't know if the snowplough driver couldn't SEE the kids in the road or just didn't CARE.

By now the snow was melting and everything was turning to SLUSH. And once the plough had left our street it was QUIET.

The crazy thing is, now that the street was ploughed, there wasn't really anything left to FIGHT over, so everyone picked themselves up and went back HOME. Even the Mingo kids went back to where they came from.

And the truth is, I couldn't really remember what we were all fighting over to BEGIN with.

Friday
We've been back at school for a week, and it's warmed up a LOT in the past few days. I don't want to curse it or anything, but I think we might've seen the last of the cold weather.

So I'm not really worried about our LOST PIG any more. In fact, he's probably somewhere warm by now, having the time of his life.

There's still some snow on the ground in my neighbourhood, so Mitchell Pickett's been enjoying the snowmobile he bought with all the money he made this winter.

So anybody who says that war doesn't PAY should think AGAIN.

Mitchell's not the ONLY one who did well, though. Trevor Nix has been playing hockey down at the bottom of the hill with the Lower Surrey Street kids every day after school. So I guess that's what you get for being a TRAITOR.

Diary of a Wimpy Kid

THE MELTDOWN

SNOW-SHOOTER

STEP 1

Tear out this page.

STEP 2

Roll up the paper to make a tube.

STEP 3

Fasten the paper with tape to secure the tube.

STEP 4

Place cotton wool or scrunched-up paper in the tube for your "snow".

STEP 5

Blow through the tube to send your snow flying!

DIARY of a Wimpy Kid THE MELTDOWN

DIARY of a Wimpy Kid THE MELTDOWN

DIARY of a Wimpy Kid THE MELTDOWN

DIARY of a Wimpy Kid THE MELTDOWN

DIARY of a Wimpy Kid THE MELTDOWN

DIARY of a Wimpy Kid THE MELTDOWN